The Grouchy Santa

The Grouchy Santa

By Lillie Patterson

Drawings by Lou Cunette

GARRARD PUBLISHING COMPANY
CHAMPAIGN, ILLINOIS

To
John and Bertha Patterson

Library of Congress Cataloging in Publication Data

Patterson, Lillie.
    The grouchy Santa.

    (First holiday books)
    SUMMARY: Mr. Grouch doesn't like Christmas and
doesn't even believe in Santa Claus until Santa takes
him around the world on Christmas Eve.
    [1. Christmas stories] I. Cunette, Lou.
II. Title.
PZ7. P2768Gr   [E]   78-21936
ISBN 0-8116-7254-9

The Grouchy Santa

Once there was a man
who was always cross.
He never smiled.
The boys and girls
called him Mr. Grouch.

Except for a servant,
he lived all alone
in a big house.
When he went for a walk,
he carried a big stick.
He would shake it
at everyone he met.
All the children were afraid
of the cross old man.
Mr. Grouch hated Christmas.
He was even more grumpy
when the holiday
came around.
He never gave
anyone a gift.
"There is no Santa Claus,"
Mr. Grouch often said.

One Christmas Eve
the old man ate supper
all by himself.
He closed his windows
to shut out the sound
of people singing
Christmas carols.

After supper
he got into bed.
He pulled his nightcap
over his head
and went to sleep.
How long he slept
he did not know.

But when he awoke
he heard a strange sound
near the fireplace.
Something was coming
down the chimney.
Mr. Grouch sat up
and lit the candle
beside his bed.
He held it high
to look around the room.
He could not believe
what he saw.
There beside the fireplace
stood Santa Claus!
"A Merry Christmas to you,
Mr. Grouch!" Santa said
in a deep voice.

Mr. Grouch was afraid.
He shook so hard
the candle wax
dripped on his hand.
"Why are you here?"
Mr. Grouch asked
in a shaking voice.

"I don't believe
in Christmas."
"But you will,"
said Santa.
"I have a special present
for you.

Put on your clothes
and be ready
before I count to ten."
Santa began counting,
"One—two—three—"
Mr. Grouch hopped
out of bed.
He got into his pants.
He tied his shoes.
Then he pulled on his coat.
He was all ready
just as Santa Claus
counted to nine.
"What is the present?"
Mr. Grouch asked Santa.
"You will find out,"
Santa replied.

A push from Santa
sent Mr. Grouch
flying up the chimney.
Santa followed close behind.
It was quiet and peaceful
on top of the house.

Snow covered everything.
In a thousand homes,
Christmas candles burned.
Suddenly, bells rang out
from churches near and far.
It was midnight.

"We must be off,"
cried Santa Claus.
His sleigh and reindeer
were waiting.
The reindeer pranced
up and down.
They were ready to go.

"Get in, get in!"
said Santa.
Mr. Grouch hopped
into the sleigh
with Santa.
The reindeer flew off
into the sky.

Away they flew
over treetops and grand houses.
"The people
who live in these homes
are rich,"
Santa told Mr. Grouch.
After a time
Santa pointed
to a small house below.
"This boy and girl
are very poor,"
Santa said.
"We will stop here first."
They landed on the roof
of the little house.
Mr. Grouch looked at Santa,
then at the chimney.

"Can we get down it?"
he asked.

"Of course,"
said Santa Claus.
"Follow me."
Down the chimney they went,
into a cold, bare room.
The fire had gone out.

Two little stockings
hung by the fireplace.
Nearby in a bed,
two children were asleep.
There was no Christmas tree.
In a corner of the room
a woman was crying.
"My poor children,"
she whispered.
"I have nothing
to give them
for Christmas."
The mother could not see
her visitors.
Santa had made
Mr. Grouch and himself
invisible.

"Her husband died
a few months ago,"
Santa Claus whispered.
"Now, see what happens."
As he spoke,
he reached into his bag.
Santa filled
each of the stockings.

He filled them with
nuts and candies,
dolls and trains,
skates and warm clothing.
When he finished,
a doll peeped out of one,
and a little train
out of the other.

Mr. Grouch held the bag
while Santa
took out more things.

They put a fat goose,
fruits, cakes, and nuts
into a basket on the floor.

Everything
the poor woman would need
for a Merry Christmas
was there.
"Now," Santa said,
"watch what happens
when she sees
all the things
we have left."
At that moment,
the mother looked up.
Her face lighted with joy.
"A magical gift bringer
has come to our home!"
she cried.
"My children will have
a Merry Christmas after all!"

"Could we wish her
a Merry Christmas?"
Mr. Grouch asked.
Santa laughed
until his fat sides shook.

"No," he said.
"She must not know
who left the presents."
Santa put his bag
over his shoulder.

He led the way
up the chimney.
All night long
Santa and Mr. Grouch
flew around the world.
Everywhere they went
they left happiness behind.

They visited children
in hospitals
and men in prisons.
They stopped
at the homes
of rich people
and poor ones.

It was a night
Mr. Grouch
would never forget.
Early in the morning,
as light showed
in the sky,
the sleigh landed
on Mr. Grouch's roof.
"Did you like
your Christmas present?"
asked Santa Claus.
"Yes," said Mr. Grouch.
"Thank you, Santa.
Now I know
what Christmas means.
I think I have found
the Christmas spirit."

On Christmas morning
the neighbors were surprised
to see Mr. Grouch
carrying a Christmas tree.
They were
even more surprised
to see that
he had been shopping.

He had
big bags of toys
and good things to eat.
Behind him
some boys and girls
skipped along the street.
Each had a toy
and a bag of candy.

"Merry Christmas to you!"
Mr. Grouch called
to everyone he met.
The old man asked
all the poor people
in the village
to come to his house.

There were presents
for everyone
under the tree.
Everyone had
a big Christmas dinner.

"Thank you, thank you,"
the people said
as they left.
"You really aren't a grouch."
They smiled at the old man.
And he smiled back.